REFLECTION OF COSMIC EMOTIONS

AKSHATA SARASWAT

NewDelhi • London

BLUEROSE PUBLISHERS
India | U.K.

Copyright © Akshata Saraswat 2024

All rights reserved by author. No part of this publication may be reproduced, stored in a retrieval system or transmitted in any form or by any means, electronic, mechanical, photocopying, recording or otherwise, without the prior permission of the author. Although every precaution has been taken to verify the accuracy of the information contained herein, the publisher assumes no responsibility for any errors or omissions. No liability is assumed for damages that may result from the use of information contained within.

BlueRose Publishers takes no responsibility for any damages, losses, or liabilities that may arise from the use or misuse of the information, products, or services provided in this publication.

For permissions requests or inquiries regarding this publication, please contact:

BLUEROSE PUBLISHERS
www.BlueRoseONE.com
info@bluerosepublishers.com
+91 8882 898 898
+4407342408967

ISBN: 978-93-5989-354-9

Cover design: Shivam
Typesetting: Namrata Saini

First Edition: June 2024

To all those who inspire me every day, whether through their actions, words, or mere presence, your influence, whether direct or indirect, is woven into the very fabric of this book. Thank you for being the guiding stars in my journey, and for your unwavering support, belief, and encouragement.

~Akshata Saraswat

Contents

Words 🍁 1

Adulting 🍼 2

Momentarily ☯ 3

What is it...? 5

Musically 🎶 6

Listen 7

Piece of peace 🕊 8

Forest Child 🌱 9

Uncertain 🍂 10

Tapestry of time ⌛ 11

Life's Projection 👣 12

Silence 🕊 13

I wish... 🌼 15

Closer 🍁 17

Entangled 🥨 18

Musing 🎶 19

Pristine Dawn 🌻 20

Falling 🍁 21

Identity 🥂 23

Collision 🦋 25

- Manmohan 🦚 26
- The dance of light ❄️ 27
- Ishq 🧕 29
- Beyond the creation ∞ 31
- Dwindling 🦇 33
- Siyavar 🏹 35
- Hold on... ⌛ 36
- Swirling 🌀 37
- Sukoon 🕊️ 39
- Rhythmic Momentum 🍀 40
- Hallucinating Night 43
- Reflection in the air 🍃 44
- The Stars ✨ 45

Words 🍁

I can feel that vibe when I write it,
I can live in that scenario when I read it,
I can get lost in it when I think about it,
I can sense its beauty, while I sit.
Words have the power to heal,
Words can show the difference between real and Reel,
Words are the best way to express,
Through words, your pain can be suppressed,
Words can make you feel calm,
While reading you can sense that warmth,
I just want to sit quietly near a river,
Covered in a blanket with a little shiver,
A pen and notepad in my hand with a liquor
While listening to the bird's chipper,
A little nearer to Fisher,
I want to deliver thoughts to that paper,
And wish to endlessly listen to her,
That's all I desire.

Adulting

And just like that,
In the lonely hours,
One more day passed.
I hope this season to change,
And meeting a soul,
Who speaks my language.
Indeed, time tells strange stories,
And leave unsaid worries,
Some stay in this silence,
Some prefer distance,
And I look for a healing space.
I know it's silly,
Hoping for something,
Something that you aren't aware,
This hope, this wait is a nightmare,
With time, this will pass,
Again, I'll stand up,
But
This time may be like a broken glass,
They say time heals everything.
After every fall,
And freezing winter,
There comes spring.
Just like that, I have realised,
As I'm growing up,
All this is a part of adulting.

Momentarily

A moment in which
Water droplets are falling,
Air is striking with subtle surroundings,
Resulting in steady trees swinging,
Darker clouds are moving,
A group of birds is flying,
The smell of wet soil is swirling,
A new life from seed is developing,
Peacocks are dancing,
This atmosphere is multitasking
While,
Someone is wondering about their existence.
Why does everything have high resistance?
Do hurdles have some magical occurrence?
Why don't reality and imagination have a coincidence?
Does that someone gets another chance?
Like the atmosphere, that moment also wanna dance.
A moment full of delusion,
A moment filled with extrusion,
A moment that's complete effusion,
A moment without happiness's fusion,
A moment that will end without any conclusion.

What is it...?

A little bit smoky
But a lot of comforts,
A little bit cozy
But more of a logical,
A little bit scary,
But full of sparks
I don't know what's it...?
But it's like my quarks,
I don't know how should I react...?
But it's like I just stay calm,
I don't know what should I say...?
But it's like I just listen,
Every time I think I'm losing it
But it's like I can't spit,
Every time I think I'm reaching to it
But it feels like I can't admit or submit,
Every time I think it's something different
But it feels like I'm just being stupid or belligerent.

Musically 🎵

While listening to that symphony,
She found her monophony,
And created a new tympany,
To get realization of that epiphany.
Its lyrical part is entirely of harmony,
Where all her chorus accompanies.
She has the sea in her soul continuously,
Deeper and beautiful simultaneously.
Her aura is made of roses and poetry.
Always dancing on the edge of mystery,
To draw a line of symmetry.
Let the waves set her free,
And write her own story.
Let her ocean consume herself wholly,
And dwell her into it gradually,
See the galaxies in her solely,
To enhance herself into a musically.

Listen

Ever tried listening to that voice,
That's trying to tell you some secrets,
Full of wicked and melancholic sounds,
Graved with bunches of choice,
Composed of the pitter-patter of hidden wounds,
Continues vibration of that whisper,
Navigating through your mind,
Resulting in heavy clouds of misery,
Followed by a flood of suffering.
Love,
Your actions are not under your guidance,
Your heart craves for the silence,
Don't let those heavy clouds take control,
Drive your life's journey with your force,
Broken doesn't mean the end,
There are still pieces left,
Though they are broken,
Still, they are beautiful.
It's just...
While admiring other's beauty,
You just forgot to see your own.

Piece of peace 🕊

Loner,
Nah!! I call it self-love,
Sitting alone in your room's window.
Listening to birds chirping under that tree's shadow,
Touching raindrops and blowing with winds flow.
watching mamma sparrow feeding baby sparrow,
Answering your mind's echo,
And planning for a better tomorrow.

I'm becoming an introvert,
But I don't want it to revert.
I'm in my desert,
Where, anything I can insert
I'm enjoying my concert,
And don't need to be alert.

I'm on a crease,
Where my emotions freeze,
My mind is on the verge of release,
And that's a true piece of peace.

Forest Child

Clocked under dark cotton candies,
Covered by pastoral beauties,
Surrounded by prominent elevations,
Whispers from the mountain blow with the air,
Echoing over the surface of the water.
This water collects memories,
Witnessing several moments over the centuries.
I sit near its banks leaving all my worries,
Quietly, I listen to the secrets,
That rain wants to tell me.
This nature sings and I dance to her ancient rhymes.
I slip into this moody forest,
Into these woods and wildflowers,
To stay rooted in nature's wind.
It treats my shadow as hers,
As I'm a forest child.

Uncertain 🍂

An unpredictable moment,
In a closed room, I spent.
There were people for acknowledgment,
But my heart isn't ready for that pigment.
My mind has become puzzled dormant,
Fulfilled with failure's scent.
My pen is out of the statement,
My beliefs are my real opponents,
But my senses aren't ready for an appointment.
My pace has no arrangement,
My activities have no excitement,
My senses are like rough cement,
My emotions have no environment,
My efforts have had no achievement,
My hopes have no exhilarating component,
My existence has no commitment .
These uncertain words are the only ingredient,
But still not sufficient,
But not enough for any investment
Just for someone's entertainment,
I'm like a saturating element,
Who is in urgent need of ointment?

Tapestry of time ⏳

And one day,
I woke up realising,
I lost that one girl,
For me who was a pearl.
In the mirth's embrace,
We shared laughter.
In fury's dance,
We shared wrath.
When shadow surrounded us,
We shared those sufferings.
But,
When I whispered,
And claimed the night to be mine,
I became venomous for her.
The night didn't see,
She is still the queen of all the stars,
I just wanted to be her pulsar,
To consume the gravity,
And set her free from all the cavities.
Love,
In the tapestry of time,
You will realise,
Even the moon has scars,
But still, it needs the night,
To bring that light,
The night might have a canvas of stars,
But Moon still wants the night to reunite,
To let the moon, shine bright,
And become an epic twilight.

Life's Projection

What is your life's definition?
An examination?
Mind's virtual imagination?
Our usual action?
Heartbeat's regulation?
Soul's satisfaction?
Or your answer depends upon the situation?
A situation with no explanation.

Life is not a race.
It's the result of that case.
When you felt relinquish or embrace.
It's hell when you don't find your space,
It's paradise when you find the right place,
There are paths that you need to trace,
There are states that you need to face,
There are moments that you need to erase,
These are your happy life's base.

Life is your thoughts or experiences,
Life is your anxiety or patience,
Life is your cessation or existence,
Life is your self-love or resistance,
Life is about your actions and their projections.

Silence

In these noisy surroundings,
brassy evening and darker welkin,
I choose to stay calm,
And want to feel your sweaty palm.
Be it Cassiopeia, Pleiades, or cloudy Andromeda,
Doesn't matter what's their lambda,
Us+telescope, that's my agenda.
Fascinated by Orion's charm,
Wrapped under your arms.
I want to get lost in that starry farm.
There is some haziness in the sky,
Maybe like me, those stars are a little shy.
All those weird shapes of constellations, I wanna apply,
Doesn't this silence sound perfect,
All these imaginations, I wanna collect,
Hoping in real life, I can reflect,
And with all this, our emotions can connect.

I wish...

In the middle of my chaos,
And contemplating the cause,
It started raindrops,
And I started thinking about eros,
Does it exist?
What does it consist of?
There must be 1000 twists,
It's full of mist.
And do I need to insist...?
I wish for a miracle,
I wish not to hustle,
I wish not to crumble,
I wish not to rumble,
I wish to be subtle,
I wish to be natural,
I wish to be a truffle,
Suddenly, the rain stopped,
And, I hoped,
What if, it all becomes true,
What will be my view,
What am I getting into,
What if I won't be able to get through?
And I will get screwed.

Closer

Come closer,
Let me look into those eyes,
And feel how our glimpses harmonize,
Let me have a taste of those soft edges,
And touch that frozen moment like a siege,
Let my hands move over your skin,
And perceive you as my sovereign.
Let my breath strike with yours,
And gasp in your every silent Converse,
Let my fingers play with those hairs,
And cure your all fears.
Let me put my head on your shoulders,
And listen to your head whispers.
Let me flow in that compact ocean,
And consume your every little notion.
Let me swallow all those rumours,
And express how it transpires.
Come closer and closer to me,
Be mine and set me free,
And run along in our deeper sea.

Entangled 🥨

It's fall and leaves are shredding from the trees,
Hot air clashes with the cold breeze.
The flower starts to squeeze,
Temperature gradually decreases,
Water starts to freeze,
That's a moment my eyes seize.

And all of this in the middle,
The world is an entangled riddle,
And I'm an unsolved puzzle,
Unaware of the path like a fiddle,
Living without a title,
Everything seemed simple,
But gradually mess is increasing a little,
My brain is acting like a wood whittle,
In which I'm drowning with slow diddle.

Fall is passing and winter is coming,
With cold air, my thoughts are freezing,
With new leaves coming,
My puzzle is not solving,
As temperature is decreasing,
My way to that path is more entangling,
New flower buds are rising,
But that wood in my brain is still whittling,
Slowly the world is changing,
But my drowning is not slowing.

Musing 🎵

A boundless feeling,
An eternity of receiving endless calming touches,
My heart smiles and my face blushes
As my thoughts won't stop orbiting around you.
My gaze tends to yours,
Searching for the ocean,
Where love never stops raining,
And can't help myself from dancing.
I can sink deeper and deeper,
In this hypothetical world of ink and paper,
And draw memories in our minds.
That's impossible to erase,
But together, those are easy to chase.
Those memories are like music,
Soft, comfy but so quick,
Let me paint colours in our world,
Let's not those memories get unfurled.
As I sing this musingly,
In the hope of becoming a musically.

Pristine Dawn

Waiting for a new dawn,
As calm as a swan,
Which flew like air blown,
But passing differently,
Filled with distinct pray,
And got answers to my every why.
By...
Fabricating the essence of serenity,
And being a conscious creator of reality.
Phrasing words in the soul of art,
Resulting in an exquisite part.
Blossoming for my joy,
And converting into a soothing alloy.
Trusting the magic of every symmetry,
And being every part of my poetry.
Cherishing the peace of pristine dawn,
And enjoying its glory like a piece of crown.

Falling

Those little reddish-brown eyes,
Continue staring like spies,
Still waiting for his tries,
And the vary next instant when I sigh,
That instant becomes my favourite high.
All those little moments till now I tie,
Suddenly became real like a surprise,
And that moment passed with some great flies.

On opening our story's pages,
Mixed with different phases,
Decorated with unforgettable praises,
Let's ink it out with some beautiful phrases.
Let's relive those moments that amaze us.
And complete our story with our interesting chases.

I know, I know, I know...
That story is never ending,
Starts with random messaging,
Continues with some weirdo's gazing,
Written with our rhyming,
And on every next page,
she found herself more falling.

everybody
grows
at
different
rates.

Identity

Who is she?
Maybe just another random confused soul,
Maybe a person with losing passion in her bowl,
Maybe a living diary that you can't scroll,
Maybe a stranger with memories of her other role,
Maybe an overthinker with lots of questions in her soul.
Sometimes, she wonders,
She has many sides, but which one is original?
She hears many voices, but which one is pinnacle?
She has many memories, but which one is liveable?
She has lots of ways, but which one is pivotal?
It seems like,
She is losing the true version of herself,
She is left alone on her bookshelf,
She is waiting for that elf,
An art that enables us to find ourselves.

Collision 🦋

Two stars collided,
To fuse into one.
Others saw the light,
We saw,
that love in our veins,
Our unchangeable reign,
That distant pain,
With that understanding, we gain.
That moment when it rains,
We, standing in the falling water,
Raindrops touching us softer than ever,
Wind blowing for every hurdle's slaughter,
Trees with mild laughter,
Clouds running a little faster,
Light coming from the canopy's border,
At that moment,
We became each other's supporters,
And you became my favourite stalker.
As for the earth, it's Jupiter,
A stalker,
Whose eyes have an affirmation,
Whose smell has some sensation,
Whose touch is full of devotion,
Whose whispers increase my affection,
Whose actions are full of obligation,
That stalker is that person who once was my imagination.

Manmohan

With the crown of *MorPankh* on this head,
Swinging under the tree's shade,
As he channels his soul and flute,
Miscellaneous things go on mute,
And surroundings blossom with his pursuit,
Endearing cows join him with his *Murli Ki Dhun*,
Yamuna stops flowing to listen to his *Venu*,
Cowgirls rush towards him leaving their chores,
Radhe comes, put her head on his shoulder,
Garnish that moment with her essence.
And every *VrindavanWasi* forgets their presence.
This moment itself is so *Manmohak*,
That, its imagination feels like flying in the *Pushpak*.
A symbol of devotion and compassion,
An epitome of knowledge,
With the breathtaking appearance,
Adored for his mischievous pranks,
Known for his perseverance,
Pouring the Earth with his presence,
Eights avatar of *Vishnu*,
Well!! Madly listening to his *Bansi* is nothing new,
That is *Kanha* for you.

The dance of light

Blended with alluring shades,
Some have their glimmer,
While some are beyond our gaze,
Owing to their diverse wavelengths.
It's scattering,
Its dispersion,
Its reflection,
Results into the Cosmic Dance.
Where beauty blooms,
As outcomes weave celestial looms.
Somewhere, above the celestial sphere,
Where shades of colours disappear and shadows sway.
Thousand light years away,
Where neutron star spins,
And cosmic ripples begin.
That travel in the fabric of space-time inn,
And,
Amidst of celestial din,
Where mysteries are deeper within.

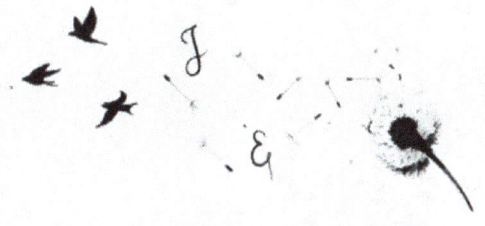

Ishq

On the banks of the holy *Ganges*,
Silently blowing cold breezes,
The serenity of flowing water,
Sailers anchoring boats,
Sitting on the antiquated *ghats*,
Representing the heritage of *Banaras*.
An ancient city,
With burning *ghats*,
With miraculous healing space,
With a rich culture,
With unique temple sculptures,
Even the streets with chaos,
Gives me the perfect cause,
To connect to my soul with a pause.
A place where *Shiv* came,
And met *Shakti*,
And gave a root to not have any *vibhakti*,
And a reason to fall into endless *prembhakti*.
They said,
"Mai Ishq likhu, tum Banaras samjhna",
Truly said.

Beyond the creation ∞

There is a deep black ocean,
Where everything is either dead or aged,
But, still, they tell us about our existence,
They are millions and billions of lightyears away,
But still, they fascinate us,
I want to watch them,
I want to understand them,
Yes, I'm talking about a magical creation.
A magical *Nisarga exists*,
And just by a look at that *Nisarga,*
You will fall in love with it.
That creation is full of mysteries,
It's the most difficult puzzle,
The more you try to solve it,
More you will get puzzled,
But there is a language of that creation,
Which was used by God to create it.
That ocean contains various bodies,
Like a steady butterfly,
A flying eagle,
A running horse,
A dark pit,
A natural lighthouse,
An attraction between two bodies,
Some swirling swings,
Some ghostly compound,

This sounds scary you know.
But these bodies and materials hold the answers to all your queries.
So, come and look beyond this creation,
That is infinitely huge,
And get lost in that dark deep ocean.

Dwindling ⭐

Dark sky and silent roads,
Still, trees swing slowly as air blows,
A scenic view I see through my window Illuminating streetlights.
Amidst that moonless night,
Resulting in the shadows of the hurdle's scattering reflection,
Like one's perception.
The shimmer of sky objects,
And their winking resemblance with one aspects,
They say,
One needs to be a star to be a supernova,
Whose vicinity and deeds should be balanced like a parabola.
At birth,
Things might be cloudy as a nebula,
You might need to find that one fibula,
That will put clouds and acts together,
 And their fusion results in a core relatively hotter.
Sometimes,
Your actions might result in hindering,
Post that, you will be twinkling,
And your surroundings will be sprinkling.
But you will start devolving and falling,
Where the gravity is dwindling.

Siyavar

Eyes as beautiful as lotus,
Arms with bow and arrows,
Whose sight can take away all the sorrows?
A dusky skinned man,
From whom this world began,
We call him *Raghuwanshi,*
Lifted *Shiv Dhanush* for *Siya,*
And unfurled endless *Prem rasiya,*
A name that *Hanuman* wrote,
And made a stone float.
Resulting in *Ram Setu,*
And *Ram* concurred evil *janhit hetu.*
Later,
Vikramaditya brought Ayodhya's glory back,
But couldn't save it from Babar's attack,
After waiting for 500 years,
Holding the tears,
Today, everyone is filled with cheers,
Because finally, we can say...
"Mere ram aa gye..."

Hold on... ⏳

Let me tell you a secret,
About my life's closet,
With lots of target,
That is safe under my blanket.
For others, I'm affable.
But my closet knows I'm a bubble.
My fellow closet is my closet's excerpt,
On which I want to hold on forever.
I want my secrets to be a silent messenger,
And become any closet character.
I'm still holding on to that one little secret.
That is safe inside my pocket.
For that those closets are passionate.

Swirling

That swirling structure
Attempting to match with the culture,
Several hazy reflections,
Transferring into distinguishable directions,
Originating from a single source,
Chasing the different forces,
That one radiating flash,
Fusing with water splash,
Constructing cryptic patterns,
Like numerous esoteric turns,
That tiny splinter,
Seeking a shelter,
And moulding the turns upside down,
Like a mysterious puzzle with a clown.
Reflections are crystallizing,
Flash isn't synthesizing,
Cryptic patterns are decrypting,
Tiny splinter isn't retarding,
The source is calming,
And that swirling structure is now settling.

Sukoon 🕊

A word that itself has a calmness,
That water droplets touching your face,
That madness in the trees of mountains,
That rolling lands of different elevations,
That chilling noise of water falling from stones,
That mysterious darkness of tunnels,
That benthic water in the lakes,
That silently blowing wind with complexions,
And your train running in between this,
What more can you ask for,
It's like a perfect moment you can store,
It's like the opening of every difficult door,
It's like a silly smile touching your heart's core,
A period in which you can explore,
A perfect time when you don't need anything anymore,
With lots of memories, you can décor,
The highest peak you can convert into shore,
And that feeling of "sukoon ke chadar" you wore.

Rhythmic Momentum 🍀

Reel or real?
A question of our life's wheel.
The action of zeal,
Now,
No need to conceal,
No need to squeal,
No need to peel,
Nothing is surreal,
Everything can heel,
Everyone can feel it.
So,
Let's dance,
And swing with the waves,
Away from those caves,
Closer to who saves,
Admire who praise.
Let's give,
A smile to a stranger,
A hug to a somber,
Some light to darker,
Hope to an outsider,
And build a beautiful browser.
Let's feel,

And be a Blooming flower,
Frame into the best structure,
nurture like a river,
Guard like a tower,
Remember those superpowers,
And swim in the history of your life's browser.

Hallucinating Night

Last night I had a dream,
We were walking by a deserted island beach.
There was peace in that environment.
And we knew together everything was within our reach.
The moon was shining bright,
You looked at me and we kissed.
Your eyes are so full of passion,
You said nothing but I understood,
We laid down and held each other,
We covered ourselves with my scarf.
But,
The tides came in and nearly covered us,
As we share a pure and beautiful love,
I had never known so much beauty,
As your skin in the pale moonlight,
Every moment is so intense and new,
On this warm, dark, and blissful night.
But as the sun rose the next morning,
You disappeared and left me alone,
I'm still on that deserted island,
Come back and bring me home.

Reflection in the air

While lying on the rooftop,
I looked at my shadow self.
It was dark all around me,
Except for that one moon ray,
I was trying to find a way.
I wanted a little adventure,
A lot of armatures,
Something to capture.
A life full of venture,
But the amidst,
I never thought of some warmth,
A feeling of mellowness,
A vibe of coziness,
The sentiment of intimacy,
That one ray was the reason for my shadow,
That's always there with me.
Its reflection in the air is the reason for my sensation,
That I'm able to feel.
Its little silver scimitar is like a trinket to me,
That I'm able to wear.
And that night is my universe,
In which I just wanna get lost.
I just wanna get lost...

The Stars

The stars are uncountable
Because they are too many
That we can't count them
The stars shine in the night
Like a diamond
They are bright in the night
I like the stars very much
Do you know,
Stars are there in the morning also
Some people didn't know
That stars are there in the morning also
I know, many things about the stars
Because I love the stars

~ Anvi Saraswat

"A small effort by my 7-year-old niece when she saw me writing down my feelings, and she tried to do the same in her own cute and unique way. She wanted me to include her words in this book. I didn't change the wording at all. So, here they are."

www.ingramcontent.com/pod-product-compliance
Lightning Source LLC
LaVergne TN
LVHW020416070526
838199LV00054B/3632